JoJo & Bow Bow

THE GHOSTESS WITH THE MOSTEST

SUPER SPECIAL

BY JoJo Siwa

nickelodeon

AMULET BOOKS
NEW YORK

Library of Congress Control Number 2021934592

ISBN 978-1-4197-5723-5

Book design by Brenda E. Angelilli

Printed and bound in U.S.A.
10 9 8 7 6 5 4 3 2 1

ABRAMS The Art of Books
195 Broadway, New York, NY 10007
abramsbooks.com

CONTENTS

CHAPTER 1

"Should I wear this shimmery white jacket, or does my outfit look better without it?" JoJo asked her best friend, Miley. JoJo was in her room, getting ready to head to a big Hollywood party with the cast of her first feature film. The actual filming wouldn't begin for several weeks, but the movie studio had set up a meet and greet for the cast. JoJo couldn't wait to meet her new castmates!

"Hmm," Miley responded as she twirled a strand of long, light brown hair around her finger. This told JoJo that Miley was deep in thought. "Your outfit looks great without the jacket," Miley continued. "But let me see it on so I can make sure that's the way to go."

JoJo nodded and pulled the lightweight bomber-style jacket over her black-and-white polka-dotted shirt. She was wearing the shirt with a sparkly pink skirt that reminded her of the type that ice skaters sometimes wore.

"Ta-da!" JoJo said, striking a pose for Miley. "What do you think?"

"It looks great both ways!" Miley exclaimed, plopping down on JoJo's bed so hard that the bed squeaked, which woke up BowBow, JoJo's adorable teacup Yorkie. "Oops, sorry, BowBow," Miley giggled. Then she turned her attention back to JoJo, who was removing the jacket so Miley could see her outfit again without it. "It's a tie," Miley said finally, throwing up her hands. "Do you have any idea how fancy the party is?"

"I don't think it's a *fancy* party," JoJo replied. "But I know we will be getting tons of pictures taken since the party is also a press event. It's being held outside, and there are supposed to be food trucks and a DJ . . . but that's pretty much all I know," JoJo explained as she perched on the bed next to Miley.

"Wow, food trucks, music, and movie stars?" Miley cried. "This sounds like the best party ever!"

JoJo grinned and nodded. She was so excited about the party that she began to bounce up and down on the bed. "I know, right? I *love* food trucks, and I just know the music is going to be amazing! This is basically going to be the best party ever . . . at least until your Halloween party in two weeks," she added quickly. "Because you seriously throw the *best* parties!"

Every year, Miley threw a Halloween party at her house, and every year the party seemed to get bigger and better. She spent weeks carefully planning it, and all that planning always paid off.

Now it was Miley's turn to bounce up and down on the bed. "I am so excited, you have no idea!"

"Oh, I think I have some idea," JoJo joked as she hopped to her feet. As much as she'd love to sit and chat more with Miley, she knew she had to finish getting ready. She walked across her room toward her walk-in closet.

"How's the party planning coming along?" she called out a few moments later from inside the closet. There was no reason she couldn't chat *and* get ready. "Were you able to secure that DJ you were looking into?"

"We're still waiting to hear back about the DJ," Miley replied. "But other than that, everything is coming along perfectly. It's going to be hard to outdo last year's party, but I'm determined to make this year's party the best ever!"

"Making it even better than last year will be no easy feat," JoJo agreed, yelling a little so Miley could hear her. "Last year's party was the bomb! But if anyone can do it, you can!"

"Aww, thanks," Miley responded. JoJo could hear in her best friend's voice that she was smiling. "But enough about my party for now," Miley went on. "Let's get back to talking about your big Hollywood party and all the movie stars you're about to meet, and then tomorrow we can start focusing on my party. Deal?"

JoJo poked her head out of the closet to give Miley a thumbs-up. "Deal! I'll be out in a second—I'm just picking out my shoes!"

"I can't believe my best friend is about to meet all these movie stars," Miley continued a moment later. "I wonder what Parker Lawrence is going to be like in real life." Parker was one of JoJo's costars. They were the same age, but this would be his fourth major movie—he was a bona fide movie star! All of JoJo's costars were.

"Hopefully, he will be really nice, since I think he'll be the only other kid on the set," JoJo replied as she emerged from her closet holding her favorite pair of glittery high-tops. She held them up to show Miley, who nodded to let JoJo know she agreed they were the perfect choice for her outfit. JoJo sat in the chair next to her desk to put the shoes on and then jumped to her feet so Miley could see her whole outfit.

"There are no other kids in the cast?" Miley asked.

"Not that I know of," JoJo replied. "So . . . what do you think? Am I paparazzi ready?"

Miley stood up from the bed and looked JoJo's outfit over carefully before declaring, "Definitely—you look great! But what did you decide about the jacket?"

"I'm not going to wear it," JoJo replied as she ran a brush through her long blond side-pony. She checked her reflection in the mirror and carefully adjusted her black bow. "Even though it's October, it's not like it's going to be cold outside, so I decided I don't need the jacket."

"Why would it be cold outside in October?" Miley asked as she sat back down on JoJo's bed. This time she was careful not to wake up BowBow, who had settled on JoJo's pillow and fallen back asleep. "The weather almost never gets cold in LA."

"I know," JoJo agreed. Even though her back was to Miley, she could see her friend reflected in the mirror. "That's what I meant . . . it's not cold here in LA in October. It's never cold here! But I'm still getting used to that. Back in Nebraska, it would be cold by now. Some years we even had to wear coats over our Halloween costumes when we went trick-or-treating!"

"You had to wear a coat over your Halloween costume?" Miley repeated, jumping up from the bed. "That sounds . . . *awful!*"

BowBow let out a little yip to let Miley know that, once again, she had disturbed her nap. But then, a moment later, she curled back up into a little ball.

JoJo laughed at the shocked expression on Miley's face. "It wasn't that big of a deal. In fact, sometimes kids would get creative and figure out ways to incorporate their jackets into their costumes. Or you could just freeze . . ."

"I would definitely go the freezing route," Miley said. Then she thought about it some more and shivered. "Or maybe not. I'm just glad we don't have to worry about that here in LA."

JoJo nodded as she dug through her jewelry box to look for the perfect bracelet to wear. She still had to figure out what her Halloween costume was going to be this year. She'd been so busy with movie stuff that she hadn't had much time to think about Halloween yet, but with it being just two weeks away, she knew she was going to have to start planning soon.

JoJo chose a pink-and-black striped enamel bracelet that she thought looked really cute with her outfit and slipped it on her wrist. Then she glanced at the alarm clock on her nightstand.

"Look at that; I'm done with five minutes to spare!"

"Let's take a few selfies," Miley suggested. "We can send them to Grace, Kyra, and Jacob."

Grace, Kyra, and Jacob were JoJo and Miley's other closest friends. JoJo was home-schooled, so she didn't go to school with the rest of the gang, but they hung out together all the time. In fact, JoJo knew she would be seeing her friends next week because they had all talked about getting together to discuss Miley's party preparations.

JoJo and Miley leaned in close while JoJo held out her phone. "Okay, let's do a smiling one first!"

The two girls beamed into the camera.

"Now let's do serious," JoJo said in a mock-serious tone. She and Miley arranged their faces into frowns but then cracked up laughing at how silly they looked.

"Stand back and let me get a few pictures of you," Miley said, gently grabbing JoJo's phone. "It will be good practice for all the paparazzi you're about to encounter."

JoJo nodded and posed as Miley snapped a few more pictures.

"These are great," she said after Miley showed the pictures to her. "I'll have to post one later for the Siwanatorz!"

Just then, JoJo's mom called upstairs to let JoJo know it was time to leave. JoJo felt an excited flutter in her stomach.

"Ready or not, I guess it's time to go," she told Miley.

"Oh, you're definitely ready," Miley assured her.

JoJo did feel ready . . . and she couldn't wait!

CHAPTER 2

A couple of hours later, JoJo was having the time of her life at the party. It was even more fun than she had dreamed it would be. Her costars were some of the nicest, friendliest people JoJo had met—especially Parker Lawrence!

The party was outside, just as JoJo had been told it would be, in a huge lot that was part of the sprawling movie studio complex. Also as promised, there were food trucks galore! So far, JoJo had sampled fare from two different trucks: the gourmet grilled cheese truck and the taco truck. She was deciding if she had room for one more thing before she moved on to dessert when Parker reappeared at her side, holding a half-eaten slice of pineapple pizza on a plate.

"There's pizza too?" JoJo cried. "How did I miss the pizza truck?"

"It's way back there." Parker grinned between bites, using his free hand to point to a truck in the far corner of the lot. "I almost missed it too. But don't worry—this is only my second piece, so there should be some left for you."

With his messy blond hair and green eyes, Parker looked like a typical kid. But when he smiled, his adorably goofy expression was the one JoJo—and most everyone else—was familiar with from the big screen.

JoJo laughed and jokingly rubbed her stomach. "I'm just not sure I have room for pizza. I need to plan carefully and save room for dessert. I don't know if there's room in there for pizza *and* dessert."

"JoJo, we have a problem," Parker said, and the smile slipped from his face.

"What?" JoJo couldn't imagine what Parker was talking about.

"I'm not sure I can be friends with you," Parker said solemnly.

"What?" JoJo repeated. "I'm pretty sure you're messing with me right now . . . but you're such a good actor I can't really tell . . ."

"I'm not messing with you," Parker said. He took a few steps back and shook his head sadly. "JoJo, I can't be friends with some-one who can't find room for pizza. I just can't . . ."

JoJo burst out laughing. She already felt like she'd been friends with Parker for a long time. He had an easygoing manner that made it very easy for her to feel comfortable around him.

Just then, JoJo's phone buzzed in her pocket.

"Do you need to get that?" Parker asked.

JoJo nodded and pulled her phone out. She glanced down at the screen. The text was from Miley:

SOOOOOO . . . HOW'S IT GOING AT THE MEET AND GREET?

"It's my best friend texting to ask how things are going," JoJo explained. "I'll just text her back to say I'll talk to her later."

JoJo dashed off a reply to Miley.

EVERYTHING GREAT HERE! WILL FILL YOU IN LATER!

Then she added a thumbs-up emoji, hit send, and placed her phone back in her pocket.

"Sorry about that," JoJo said.

"No problem," Parker replied easily. He wiped his mouth with a napkin and folded up the empty paper plate that had, moments ago, contained the slice of pizza. "What's your BFF's name?"

JoJo filled Parker in on Miley and then told him a bit about Kyra, Grace, and Jacob.

"Sounds like a great crew," Parker commented.

"They really are," JoJo agreed. "How about you? Who's your best friend?"

"His name is Ethan," Parker replied. "We've been friends since preschool. I don't get to see him a lot lately since I moved to LA and made three movies in the past two years, but when I'm visiting my grandparents back home and we can be together, we have some pretty amazing Xbox competitions!"

"That's so neat," JoJo replied.

"He's really into Halloween, and we have had some truly fantastic trick-or-treat adventures," Parker continued. JoJo noticed

Parker's face lit up as he talked about his friend. "One year I filled up three pillowcases with candy! We used to go trick-or-treating for *hours* in a bunch of different neighborhoods. One year we even changed costumes midway through—we did afternoon costumes, went home to rest and refuel, and then changed into scarier costumes for nighttime trick-or-treating."

"That's an awesome idea," JoJo said, thinking she'd have to mention it to her friends. She told Parker how much Miley loved Halloween and about her upcoming Halloween party.

Just then, a photographer approached them. "JoJo and Parker, can I get a quick shot of the two of you?" she asked.

"Of course," JoJo moved closer to Parker so they could pose together. JoJo held her smile as the camera's very bright flash went off a few times.

"And now I'm seeing spots," Parker said as the photographer thanked them and moved on. "What were we talking about?"

"Halloween parties," JoJo reminded him.

"Right! I love a good Halloween party!" Parker said enthusiastically. "It gives me a chance to show off my costume skills. I basically have the best costume *every* Halloween. Especially when it comes to the spooky ones."

JoJo raised her eyebrows.

"What, you think I'm joking?" Parker asked.

"No, I think you probably *think* you have the best costume," JoJo said, biting her lip to keep from laughing at the expression on Parker's face. "And I'm sure your costumes are nice and everything . . ." She let her voice trail off as Parker pretended to get really mad.

"Oh, and I suppose your costume game is perfectly on point?" Parker asked.

"Pretty much," JoJo shrugged.

"JoJo Siwa, is that a challenge?" Parker whooped. "I feel like you just challenged me! What do you say we make a bet to see who can come up with the better Halloween costume this year?"

"I never say no to a challenge," JoJo said quickly. "But how would that work?"

Before Parker could answer, a girl who appeared to be a few years older than them approached with a warm smile on her face.

"This discussion is to be continued," Parker whispered, and JoJo laughed.

"Sorry to interrupt, but I wanted to come say hello," the girl said. She had long, dark brown hair with bright blue streaks that she wore in braids. "I'm Lana Marks. My dad is working on your movie. I'm a big fan of both of yours!"

"It's so nice to meet you, Lana," JoJo replied. She loved meeting her fans. She looked at Parker, who was smiling but actually looked a little bit nervous. JoJo decided to keep talking. "This party is so great, isn't it? My only complaint is that I didn't come hungrier—I wish I could try something from every food truck!"

"I know, right?" Lana agreed. "But if you only have room for one more thing, make sure you try a candy apple from Mo's Candy Apples truck," Lana pointed to a bright yellow truck with candy and caramel apples painted all over it. "They're my favorite fall dessert! I promise you these are the best ones you will ever taste. When my dad told me there were going to be food trucks here, I told him he *had* to get a Mo's truck."

"Thanks for the tip," JoJo replied. "A candy apple actually sounds perfect. I was debating about what to get for dessert, but now it's settled."

Just then, another photographer approached them.

"Lana, can we get a shot of you with Parker and JoJo?" the photographer asked.

"Sure, if you want to," Lana agreed. She turned to JoJo and flashed a big bright smile. "No candy apple in my teeth, right?"

"You're good!" JoJo assured her.

The three new friends leaned in together and smiled as the photographer snapped several shots.

"I think his flash was even brighter than the last one," Parker said, jokingly opening and closing his eyes in an exaggerated way.

The three of them chatted for a few more minutes, exchanging numbers so they could keep in touch, before Lana gracefully excused herself. "I think I see my dad waving me over to him, so I have to go, but it was so nice meeting both of you. I'll talk to you soon, I hope."

"She was super nice," JoJo commented to Parker as Lana walked away. They headed over in the direction of the candy apple truck to get in line. "I wonder who her dad is. She said he works on our movie but then also said he had a hand in choosing the trucks for the party. So maybe he's in food services?"

"JoJo, do you not know who Lana is?" Parker asked.

JoJo shook her head as the line moved forward. "No. Is she an actress or a model?"

"No, she's . . ." Parker paused as if he was trying to figure out how to explain who Lana was. "She's basically . . . Hollywood royalty! Her dad is the producer of our movie, and her mom is Jade Rio."

"Her mom is Jade Rio?" JoJo repeated. She definitely knew who Jade Rio was . . . she was one of the biggest movie stars in the world "I had no idea! Wow, I can't wait to tell my friends! Grace is basically obsessed with Jade Rio. She's going to flip when I tell her I met her daughter. And that she was so friendly!"

"She really was," Parker agreed. "Lana is pretty famous in her own right. I was a little starstruck meeting her at first. Thanks for covering for me by keeping the convo going."

"No problem," JoJo shrugged. "Especially since I didn't know who she was to get starstruck."

They were almost to the head of the line. "I'm kind of dying to find out what makes these candy apples so spectacular, but I think I might get mine to go so I can try the Froyo stand," Parker said.

"Parker, we have a problem," JoJo said. She fixed a stern expression on her face and crossed her arms. Parker raised his eyebrows.

"I can't be friends with someone who can only handle one dessert," JoJo said finally.

Parker burst out laughing as he ordered one candy apple to go.

"I'll take mine to go too," JoJo told the woman standing at the window. "Actually, can I get more than one?"

"Sure. How many would you like?" the woman asked.

"Hmm. Can I get three?" JoJo asked.

The woman nodded and a few moments later handed JoJo a yellow paper bag with MO'S CANDY APPLES written on the front in fancy red script.

"You weren't kidding about saving room for dessert!" Parker joked as they walked away from the truck.

"These are not all for me," JoJo chuckled. "I wanted to get extras so I can share with my friends. We'll be getting together next week to help Miley plan her Halloween party."

"Right, the party you'll be wearing the costume to that will *not* be able to beat my superior Halloween costume?" Parker asked, a mischievous smirk on his face.

"You just keep on going with your trash talk." JoJo returned his smirk.

"Unless you've realized you can't possibly win and want to chicken out," Parker said, a taunting edge to his voice.

"Definitely not chickening out," JoJo assured him. "We need to figure out how we're doing this and who will be the judge and all that."

Parker nodded excitedly. JoJo could tell she was going to have her work cut out for her trying to come up with a costume that would beat Parker's. He was obviously extremely competitive when it came to Halloween costumes.

"Agreed—we will have to give some thought to who will be the judge. But we can sort that out. Just let me know for sure if you're in or not. Because once you say yes, I will hold you to it!"

"Oh, I'm in," JoJo said. Her mind was already whirling with ideas for the best costume to win the competition. "I'm so in!"

CHAPTER 3

When JoJo returned home from the party that night, the first thing she did was send a group text to Miley, Kyra, Grace, and Jacob to see if they could come over after school the next day. They had so much to catch up on—not to mention party planning and candy apple sampling!

Luckily, it didn't take long for all their responses to come in—and their after-school meetup was set!

A little while later, JoJo was relaxing in her room with BowBow and getting ready for bed when her phone pinged. She picked it up, expecting to see a text from Miley, but it was actually from Parker.

HI NEW FRIEND! FIGURED OUT YOUR COSTUME YET?

JoJo dashed off a reply.

COSTUME STILL IN THE WORKS BUT HAVE CALLED IN REINFORCE-MENTS—FRIENDS ARE COMING OVER TOMORROW FOR COSTUME PLANNING SESH!

They went back and forth a few more times, with Parker playfully teasing JoJo that her odds of coming up with a better costume than his didn't sound very good if she was already calling in reinforcements.

JoJo replied:

HAVEN'T U EVER HEARD FIVE HEADS ARE BETTER THAN ONE?

Moments later, Parker's response came back:

IS THAT YOUR COSTUME? FIVE-HEADED MONSTER? I'VE GOT THIS IN THE BAG!

JoJo was still laughing as she put her phone down. She wished there was a way her friends could somehow meet Parker—she knew they'd like him as much as she did.

"JoJo, if you don't start giving me the details on what every celebrity was wearing at the meet and greet, I might explode," Kyra said as she reached for a mini cupcake. "Start with Lana Marks. I can't believe you met her. She's basically Hollywood royalty, you know . . . and her fashion sense is impeccable at every red-carpet event!"

It was the next afternoon, and JoJo's friends—minus Grace, who had not arrived yet—were gathered in JoJo's backyard, just past the pool, near the trees at the edge of the yard. It was an uncharacteristically cloudy day and a bit too chilly to go swimming, but

JoJo thought the weather was actually pretty perfect for hanging outside.

"Parker said the same thing about Lana being Hollywood royalty," JoJo replied to Kyra. "And you are right about her fashion sense—her outfit was pretty awesome . . ." JoJo described the white jeans and oversize off-the-shoulder striped shirt Lana had been wearing. "Her hair was actually kind of similar to yours, with colored streaks, but her streaks were blue."

Kyra grinned and swept her long, dark, purple-streaked hair behind her shoulder. "So I almost have the same hair as a Hollywood fashion icon?"

"Well . . . hers was also braided. But sure, why not!" JoJo laughed.

"Hmph," Kyra grumbled. But then she laughed too. She was only pretending to be upset.

"These cupcakes are yummy," Jacob commented, licking orange frosting from his thumb. "It's tricky to get this much color in the icing without affecting the flavor, but this is really good."

Jacob was a fantastic baker who had even competed in a big baking championship. He was the best kid baker JoJo knew.

"I'm glad you approve," JoJo said. "I thought about also serving hot apple cider to tie in with the whole fall vibe, but it's not quite cool enough for hot apple cider today."

"It's actually a *little* chilly out here today," Miley commented as she reached for her hoodie. "If I close my eyes, I can almost imagine it's the kind of fall you said you had in Nebraska, JoJo . . ."

"Oh, fall in Nebraska is chillier than this," JoJo replied. "Also, fall in Nebraska has its own smell, and it's very different from the smell of fall in LA."

"Wait, fall is *scented*?" Jacob asked, frowning.

"It's hard to explain," JoJo giggled. She looked at Miley and Kyra. "Back me up. You know what I mean, right?"

"I think so," Miley nodded. "Stop being so difficult, Jacob," she added jokingly.

Jacob laughed. "I was just thinking . . . if I knew exactly what fall smelled like, maybe I could capture the taste in a perfect dessert to bring to your Halloween party."

"In that case, you may proceed with your questions," Miley replied. "Let's see . . . to me, fall smells like pumpkin spice candles!"

"Or maybe pumpkin spice lattes," Kyra added.

"Pumpkin spice *everything!*" JoJo cheered as everyone started talking about their favorite pumpkin spice creations.

"What'd I miss?"

JoJo looked up to see Grace rushing out toward them. Her long red hair was held back from her face with a velvet headband, and JoJo could see there was a bright smile on her face.

She quickly filled Grace in on what they had been discussing as Grace helped herself to a cupcake and a beverage.

"I'm actually not a huge pumpkin fan," Grace admitted as she opened her can of sparkling water. "Not even pumpkin pie at Thanksgiving."

"Hey, to each their own," JoJo said. "What fall flavor do you love the most?"

"Probably apple," Grace said as she nibbled on her cupcake. "Apple spice, caramel apple, candy apple . . . I love all the apples!"

"That reminds me!" JoJo exclaimed. "I have a little surprise for you all. Be right back!"

When she returned from the kitchen a few moments later, JoJo was carrying a platter with the candy apples from the food truck at the party. Her mom had sliced two up to share but left one apple whole so everyone could see it in all its shiny, red, sticky glory.

"Oh my gosh, I love candy apples—and those look amazing!" Miley cried as JoJo set the platter down. "Where did you get them?"

"One of the food trucks at the party was a candy and caramel apple truck," JoJo explained. "Lana Marks said these are her faves, so I brought some home thinking we could all try them together."

"I can't believe I'm about to eat something that is a favorite food of Lana Marks, daughter of my favorite actress!" Grace exclaimed as she reached for a piece of apple. "Has anyone ever told you that you are the greatest friend in the world? Thank you so much for sharing with us!"

"I'm happy I could bring a little bit of the party home to you all," JoJo said as everyone took their first bite.

"Jacob, you were wondering before what fall might taste like?" Miley said a moment later. "It's this candy apple here. Perfectly fall. Perfectly yummy. In fact, this just gave me an idea . . ." Miley paused dramatically.

"Don't keep us in suspense!" JoJo cried. "What's your idea?"

"I'm going to try to get the candy apple truck to come to *my* party!" Miley announced. "Won't that be terrific? JoJo, do you remember the name of the truck?"

"It was Mo's Candy Apples," JoJo told her.

"Awesome!" Miley pulled out her phone and dashed off a text. "Just asking my mom to look into booking the Mo's truck for the party," she explained.

"So speaking of your party . . ." JoJo nodded at her BFF. "We need an update on how everything is coming along."

"Right . . ." Miley began digging through her backpack. She retrieved an orange spiral notebook and held it up for everyone to see. "This is my party planning notebook," she explained.

"Wow, you are seriously organized!" Kyra commented. "Not to mention color-coordinated, which I of course approve of."

Miley opened her notebook and began looking over her notes. "Well, one thing that's totally done is the Monster's Laboratory my dad and uncle are creating in the basement. They are both dressing up in scary costumes—my dad is going to be a vampire—and they are doing an interactive game."

"What's that?" JoJo asked.

"I think I know," Grace said, inching forward in her chair. "It's where the guests are blindfolded and asked to touch all sorts of yucky things in bowls, and the monsters tell you you're touching things like intestines and eyeballs from their lab, right?"

As Miley nodded, Kyra gasped.

"Ew, gross! I am not touching intestines or eyeballs!" Kyra cried.

"They're not real," Miley assured her between giggles. "It's stuff like . . . peeled grapes and cooked spaghetti noodles. They just feel gross because you're blindfolded."

"Oh, okay," Kyra said slowly. "Still not sure I'll be doing that."

"Count me in," JoJo cheered.

"Me too!" Jacob added.

Just then, Miley's phone buzzed.

"Oh, that might be my mom responding already about the candy apple truck," Miley said. But as she glanced at the screen, her face fell.

"What's wrong?" JoJo and Grace asked at the same time.

"It was my mom, but she was texting to tell me that we can't get the DJ we wanted for the party. He's already booked for some other big party that night."

"Oh, that stinks," Jacob said. "I'm sorry, Miley."

"Yeah, I know you really wanted that DJ," Grace added sympathetically.

Miley shrugged, but JoJo could tell she was upset.

"I have an idea," JoJo said suddenly. "Why don't we come up with an amazing play-list and stream music from an iPad? Great dance music is great dance music, right?"

"That could totally work," Kyra agreed. "My dad has really high-quality speakers, and I'm sure he'll let you borrow them . . ."

"Yeah, maybe," Miley nodded. "Thanks so much. I really appreciate the offer. I'll definitely think about it . . ."

Even though she had a small smile on her face, JoJo could tell Miley was still disappointed. "It's going to be spectacular, no matter what!" she assured Miley. "Siwanatorz never give up, right?"

"Right!" Miley nodded again. But now her smile was brighter. She made a quick note in her notebook. "You know what? You're right—streaming music on an iPad will work great! I'll talk to my mom about it. And Kyra, if you could talk to your dad about the speakers, I'd really appreciate it."

"On it," Kyra responded, whipping out her own phone to text her dad.

"That's the spirit!" JoJo cheered. "Okay, so who wants to head inside for some pumpkin painting?"

"I'm in!" Jacob cried.

"Me too!" Grace and Miley said in unison, jumping up from their chairs.

Only Kyra remained frozen in her chair, her eyes fixed on the trees at the edge of the yard. "There's . . . there's something lurking in the trees over there," she said in a shaky voice.

"Kyra, that's not funny," Grace began. But then her voice faltered. "Wait, I think I saw something move over there too," she whispered.

"See, I told you!" Kyra cried, jumping up from her chair and rushing to Grace's side.

"Maybe we should just go inside," Jacob said slowly.

"C'mon, I'm sure it's nothing," JoJo assured her friends. But then she heard a rustling sound and was pretty sure she caught a flash of movement near the trees. "I'm going to go check it out."

"No, wait!" Miley cried. "What if it's ... a ghost or something?"

"It's definitely not a ghost!" JoJo was 99 percent sure. "But even so ... does anyone want to come with me?"

"Siwanatorz always stick together," Miley replied, stepping forward. And then Jacob, Grace, and Kyra stepped forward too. The five of them linked arms and slowly tip-toed to the edge of JoJo's yard.

A moment later Kyra let out a terrified shriek ... and then as she and the others realized what was moving in the trees, they all doubled over laughing.

CHAPTER 4

"I cannot believe you people were so scared of a bunny!" Kyra said. "A cute, adorable, fuzzy little bunny. It was as small and harmless as BowBow!"

JoJo and her friends were sprawled out at the kitchen table, first drawing faces on their pumpkins using washable markers before painting them.

"Um, who screamed like she was auditioning for a role in a horror movie?" Jacob replied, doing a hilarious imitation of Kyra's scream when she spotted the bunny darting out of the trees. JoJo, Grace, and Miley couldn't help but crack up laughing.

Kyra stuck her tongue out but then dissolved into laughter too. "Okay, you're right. I might have overreacted just a teeny bit!"

"It's all good," JoJo assured Kyra. "A little scare like that is perfect for this time of year. Like this . . ." JoJo turned her pumpkin around to show everyone the scary ghost face she'd drawn on it. "Back in Nebraska, it was a tradition in my neighborhood to try to come up with the spookiest-looking pumpkins and then decorate your front steps with them. One house would be scarier than the next. It was so awesome!"

"What were some of your other fall traditions in Nebraska?" Miley asked.

JoJo thought about it for a moment. "Well, one of my favorite things to do was a haunted hayride. We'd go on one every year at the local pumpkin patch."

"What exactly is a haunted hayride?" Kyra asked.

"Hang on," JoJo said. She pulled out her phone and began typing away.

"I know that look," Miley said as JoJo continued to type, an excited gleam in her eyes.

"Aha! Found one!" JoJo cried. She looked up from her phone and beamed at her friends. "I just googled it, and there are no pumpkin farms around here, but there is a strawberry farm not too far away that does haunted hayrides. Rather than me try to explain it to you, you can experience it yourself. Let's all go one night this week!"

"That sounds awesome!" JoJo's friends exclaimed.

"I can't wait to share one of my favorite fall traditions with you," JoJo said happily.

For a few minutes, it was quiet around the table as everyone concentrated on drawing their pumpkin faces, but then Jacob broke the silence. "So, we're supposed to be planning Halloween costumes, right? Does anyone have their costume picked out yet?"

"Oh! Speaking of Halloween costumes . . . I can't believe I almost forgot to tell you something!" JoJo said excitedly. She placed the cap back on the marker she'd been using and put it on the table next to her pumpkin. "I kind of have a bet going with Parker Lawrence about who can come up with the best costume. He claims he's the king of costumes, and I couldn't say no when he basically dared me to try to come up with a better costume this year!"

"Oh, you so have to win!" Kyra cheered.

"I know right?" JoJo grinned as she tapped the marker on the table. "I still haven't figured out my costume, but it's going to have to be really good to beat him. You should have heard him bragging about how great his costumes are every year! He even teased me about wanting to chicken out from competing against him."

"What?" Jacob yelled in mock horror. "He clearly does not know you very well. JoJo Siwa does not back down from a challenge!"

"Exactly!" JoJo laughed.

"Do you have *any* idea of what you want to dress up as?" Grace asked. "Maybe we can all help you come up with something amazing to beat him."

"Well . . ." JoJo began.

"Hang on, I just had another idea," Miley said slowly. "What if I have a costume contest at my party? Parker can livestream in for the judging, or he can send us a Snapchat video, and then he can be in the contest too! All I need to do is come up with an amazing prize for the winner . . ."

"I love that idea, Miley!" JoJo exclaimed. She was so excited she jumped up from her chair and began to pace around the kitchen. "I can't wait to tell him. Where's my phone? I'm going to text him right now!"

As JoJo dashed off a text to Parker, Jacob sneaked a peek at Grace's pumpkin and let out an excited whoop. "Wow, Grace, that's so good!"

"Show us!" JoJo cried, quickly hitting send and putting her phone down on the table.

"I didn't go the spooky route," Grace said shyly, turning her pumpkin around to show everyone. JoJo was not surprised to see that Grace had drawn a unicorn. She was basically obsessed with them.

Grace's unicorn was extremely detailed. It had a pink and blue mane and the sweetest face.

"Wow, Grace, your art skills just keep getting better and better," Miley said.

"For sure," JoJo agreed. Grace was the best artist JoJo knew. "That looks professional."

"That's it!" Kyra cried suddenly, throwing her marker down. "There's your costume contest prize, Miley! A pumpkin painted by Grace! She can paint a picture of whatever the winning costume is on a pumpkin for the winner."

"What a great idea," Miley agreed. "Grace, would you do that for me?'

"Well, sure I would," Grace said slowly. "But do you really think that's a good enough prize?"

"Are you kidding? It's a *fabulous* prize," Kyra said, and the rest of the group nodded.

"Then I'd love to do it," Grace said, a blush coloring her cheeks.

"And I love that sharing one of my Nebraska traditions helped solve a dilemma for Miley's party," JoJo added.

"Wait, I just thought of something," Kyra said, holding up a hand. "If we are all competing against Parker in the contest, we're also competing against each other, right? So that means . . ."

"We have to keep our costumes secret," JoJo and Miley said at the same time.

"Ugh, that's going to be really hard to do," Grace groaned. But then a broad smile lit up her face. "But I'm in!"

"Me too," Kyra agreed.

Miley and Jacob nodded.

"This is the best idea ever!" JoJo said excitedly as her phone pinged. "Hang on, I think Parker just wrote back."

As JoJo looked at her phone again, more closely this time, she realized she had a missed call from Parker. And a text that said CALL ME ASAP!

JoJo told her friends about the missed call and the text. "Should I Facetime him so you can all meet him?"

"That would be great," Miley said as she reached into her backpack. "But here—use my tablet so we can see him better!"

JoJo quickly texted Parker to let him know the plan. Parker wrote back with the thumbs-up emoji.

Moments later, Parker's face filled the screen on Miley's tablet. JoJo introduced each of her friends, turning the tablet so Parker could see everyone.

"I feel like I know each of you already," Parker said as he smiled and waved. But then his expression turned a little more serious. "So, look, JoJo, I have some news,"

Parker said. "Have you checked your texts recently?"

"Nope, I've been hanging out with everyone for the past couple of hours," JoJo replied. "Why? What's up?"

"Lana Marks is throwing a big party the night before Halloween, and she invited us. As you know, her dad is the producer for our movie, so the entire cast is invited. It will be great press for the film, and I'm sure it's expected that we will all attend . . . but I know you already have plans, with Miley's party happening that night too . . ." Parker bit his lip nervously.

JoJo looked around at her friends. They all appeared as nervous as Parker—except Miley, who was sporting a brave smile.

"JoJo, you should totally go to Lana's party," Miley said firmly. "It sounds really important for the movie. And besides, it's Lana Marks! How can you say no?"

"You're even more awesome than JoJo said you were." Parker's smile filled the screen. "JoJo, I do agree with Miley. It's probably pretty important that you come to Lana's party. What are you going to do?"

"It's not even a question," JoJo said. It looked like all of her friends, including Parker, were holding their breath. "I will just let Lana know that my best friend is having a Halloween party that same night, and I can't miss it. I'm sure she will understand. It's really not that big of a deal!"

"You can't miss a party that Lana Marks is throwing to come to my party—" Miley began.

"Of course I can," JoJo shrugged. "You're my best friend, and I promised you I'd be there. Not to mention, I *want* to be there! I'm sure Lana's party will be great and all, but Miley, I wasn't kidding when I said no one throws a better Halloween party than you. I'm sure there will be other press opportunities."

"Aww, group hug!" Kyra cried, jumping up from her chair.

JoJo laid the tablet down on her own chair as she stood up to hug her friends. She knew she had made the right decision.

"Hello? What am I missing?" Parker cried from the tablet. "Everything just went dark! Did someone mention a group hug?"

JoJo giggled as everyone sat back down, and she held the tablet up again so Parker could see everyone. "Sorry about that!"

"It's okay," Parker said. But he had a sad look on his face. "I'm bummed that you won't be at Lana's party with me," Parker said solemnly. "Partly because it would be so much fun to hang out again." He paused, and a wicked smile lit up his face. "But also because it would be great for you to see my awesome costume so I could show you in person how much better it is!"

"And here we go again," JoJo laughed, throwing up her hands. "About that . . . I have an update for you on our costume contest. It just got a whole lot bigger!"

Miley quickly explained that she'd decided to have a costume contest at her party and that if Parker agreed to participate by sending a Snapchat video, he could be judged against everyone else at the party. "Unless . . ." Miley finished, her mouth twitching as she tried not to laugh. "You're scared to compete against so many others? Are you maybe . . . *chicken?*"

"Oh no you didn't just call me a chicken!" Parker cried as JoJo cracked up. "It's so on!"

CHAPTER 5

That night, a few hours after her friends left, JoJo received a mysterious text from Kyra inviting her to come over the next day after school to discuss something "top-secret." JoJo couldn't imagine what it could possibly be, but she had a sneaking suspicion it must have *something* to do with Halloween.

The next day flew by for JoJo in a blur of homeschooling lessons, dance practice, acting lessons, pulling together a playlist of her favorite dance songs for Miley, and looking at Halloween costumes on Instagram for inspiration.

And then it was time to head over to Kyra's. Her mom had come to pick JoJo up on her way home from work. It was a quick ride to Kyra's house. Kyra was waiting at the front door when they pulled into the driveway.

"Hi Mom! Hi JoJo!" Kyra waved. "Let's grab some snacks and head out back. It's gorgeous outside." JoJo thanked Kyra's mom for the ride, and then the girls headed for the kitchen at the rear of the house. "How do pretzels and hummus sound?"

"Perfect," JoJo replied.

"There are some bottles of apple cider in the fridge if you want to make things even more fall friendly," Kyra added, gesturing to the refrigerator.

Once the girls were settled at the patio table on the back deck, JoJo decided she couldn't wait a moment longer. "Sooo . . . what's the top-secret thing you texted me about?"

"Oh, right!" Kyra laughed as she loosened the cap on her bottle of apple cider. "I figured you would have guessed it!"

"How would I guess it?" JoJo exclaimed. "You gave me no clues! I'm thinking it must have something to do with Halloween . . .?"

"You're warm," Kyra said, shimmying her shoulders back and forth.

"Um . . . does it have to do with the costume contest?" JoJo asked.

"Warmer," Kyra replied.

"Hmm . . ." JoJo tried to figure out the secret surprise, but there were just so many possibilities! "Can you give me a hint?" she asked as she piled a few pretzels on a plate.

"Sure thing," Kyra said. "It has to do with *Grace's* costume.

"Wait, did she tell you what she's going to be?" JoJo asked.

Kyra shook her head. "But think about it. What is Grace's all-time favorite thing?"

It took JoJo less than a second to respond. "Unicorns!"

"*Ding-ding-ding!*" Kyra cheered. "I figured there's a really good chance she'll dress up as a unicorn, so I'm going to make her a fabulous unicorn horn for her costume!"

"That's fantastic!" JoJo replied excitedly. Kyra, a budding fashion designer, was especially skilled at creating unique accessories.

JoJo munched thoughtfully on a pretzel. "But what if she's not a unicorn? Then what?"

"Then she will have an awesome horn to wear some other time!"

"I love it!" JoJo nodded. And she really did. Kyra was such a wonderful friend. "But what do you need my help for?"

"Well, part of it was I just wanted to tell someone, and I know you can keep a secret," Kyra giggled. "But also I wanted your advice on what color I should make the horn. What if I design a horn that *doesn't match?*"

Kyra looked so horrified at the thought of a mismatched horn that JoJo had to bite her lip to keep from laughing. "I'm sure it will look great no matter what," JoJo said reassuringly. "I mean, maybe not if you make it . . . I don't know, *brown.* But I think you can choose any color of the rainbow and you'll be good to go!"

"JoJo, you're a genius!" Kyra shouted, jumping up from her chair in excitement. "That's it! Thank you so much!"

JoJo was totally confused. "Um, what'd I say? Other than not to make it brown?"

"RAINBOW!" Kyra looked at JoJo as if it was the most obvious thing in the world. "I'll make a rainbow glitter horn that will match with *everything!*"

JoJo smiled. A rainbow glitter horn did sound perfect . . . not to mention super cute.

"Glad to be of service," JoJo said, taking a swig of apple cider.

As the conversation turned to Miley's party, Kyra said that her dad had agreed to loan Miley and her family his speakers for the party. "That was a great idea you had about the music," she added.

"I'm glad it worked out with the speakers," JoJo replied as she reached for a few more pretzels. "I sent Miley a playlist this afternoon too, so it sounds like the music should be all set."

"So, did you respond to Lana yet?" Kyra asked a moment later.

"Yep, I messaged her last night and explained about Miley's party," JoJo replied. "She responded this morning and she totally understood, so we're all good."

"That's great," Kyra nodded. "I still kind of can't believe you're missing it . . . but I'm really glad you'll be with us!"

"I'm glad I will too," JoJo said. "Miley's parties are the best, and there's no one I'd rather spend Halloween eve with than all of you!"

"Even though it means missing out on the chance to do press for your movie?" Kyra asked.

JoJo nodded. "Like I said last night, there will be other opportunities for press stuff. My friends come first."

"I know it's probably not easy, but you're so good at balancing everything," Kyra said as she drained the last of her apple cider. "You're an awesome friend."

JoJo smiled. It wasn't always easy, but her friends were worth it.

Later that evening, JoJo was back at home and digging through her mom's crafting closet to look for Halloween costume inspiration. There were enough supplies in there to fill a small store. She saw some beautiful silky fabric in shades of blue and green that reminded her a bit of peacock feathers. For a moment, she considered a peacock costume. She imagined how spectacular the silky feathers would be, especially if they were bedazzled with colorful rhinestones. She was *very* tempted by the idea. She did like peacocks, and in the back of her mind she realized she'd always kind of wanted to dress up as one because of how colorful they were . . . but was a peacock costume special enough to win the contest? JoJo wasn't sure.

After dinner, JoJo helped her mom set things up so the family could carve pumpkins together. This was something they did every year, and JoJo loved it.

JoJo decided to go the scary route once again with another ghost face. First, she drew the outline with a washable marker, and then, once it was perfect, she carefully carved out the details to make the face.

When she was finished, JoJo peered carefully at it.

"It needs something," JoJo murmured as she inspected it. "Hey Mom, can we put a candle inside?"

JoJo's mom nodded and went inside to find a candle and some matches.

A few minutes later, with her mom's help, JoJo carefully placed a candle inside her pumpkin. Once the candle was lit, a warm, eerie glow came from inside the pumpkin, illuminating the ghost face JoJo had carved on it. Now it was perfect.

"It's so spooky. I love it!" JoJo exclaimed.

As she looked at her ghostly jack-o'-lantern, JoJo realized something: She wanted a spooky costume for the party. An idea was beginning to form in her mind. Just as her almost-perfect carved pumpkin needed a little something extra to make it perfectly spooky, maybe that's what her costume needed.

"That's it!"

Her family looked at her in confusion, and JoJo laughed. "Did I say that out loud? Sorry, I think I just figured out my Halloween costume. Well, sort of . . ." She turned to her mom. "Remember how we used to go on haunted hayrides at the pumpkin patch in Nebraska? Well, I found a strawberry farm

66

not far from here that does something similar. I was thinking it would be so great to go one night with Miley, Kyra, Grace, and Jacob. What do you think?"

"I love that you're sharing our old Nebraska traditions with your friends," JoJo's mom replied. "Of course I can take you."

JoJo was more excited about the haunted hayride than ever before because maybe . . . just maybe . . . it would give her the inspiration she needed for the perfect spooky costume that was starting to take shape in her mind.

CHAPTER 6

A few days later, Miley was at JoJo's house getting ready to leave for the strawberry farm, where they would be meeting up with Grace, Kyra, and Jacob for the *spooktacular* haunted hayride.

"I'm thinking tonight's the night," JoJo told her friend. "If this hayride doesn't give me inspiration for my costume, I don't know what will!" She grabbed a brush from her dresser and slowly ran it through her long side-pony. The bow she'd chosen for tonight was red, yellow, and orange plaid. It matched nicely with her orange tee and black leggings.

"Oooh, does this mean you are thinking of doing something spooky?" Miley asked, her eyes twinkling. She walked over to JoJo's dresser, picked up a bedazzled headband, and tried it on. "I'm guessing you won't give me any hints? And what do you think—headband or no headband?"

"No headband," JoJo said decisively. "Your hair looks great just like that. And definitely no hints!"

Miley laughed and flopped down on JoJo's bed. "Not talking about our costumes is way harder than I expected it to be."

JoJo shrugged and mimicked zipping her lips closed. "I'm not spilling any beans," she said through closed lips.

"Fine," Miley pretended to pout but then started to laugh. "Any word from Parker recently?"

"We've been texting a bunch," JoJo said as she began to rummage through her dresser drawers. "He's sent me pictures of some of his costumes from past years, and I have to say, he wasn't kidding when he said he's got some serious skills."

"Between the five of us, someone has got to come up with something that can beat him," Miley said. Then she paused to look at the growing heap of clothes on JoJo's floor. "What are you looking for?"

"My black sweater," JoJo sighed. "With the orange stripes? It'll be perfect for the haunted hayride because it's soft and cuddly. You know the one I mean?"

Miley giggled and pointed to a sweater that was draped over the back of JoJo's desk chair. "You mean that one?"

"Yes!" JoJo squealed, running over to grab the sweater and slip it on over her T-shirt. "Now we can leave!"

"I think we'd better clean up first!" Miley hopped off the bed to begin picking up clothes and folding them.

"Whoops, good call." JoJo followed suit. "What would I do without you?"

A half hour later, JoJo, Miley, Grace, Kyra, and Jacob were waiting in a very long line at the farm. There was a slight fall chill in the air, and it was already dark outside. Truly the perfect setting for a haunted hayride!

JoJo's mom and Kyra's mom waved from the outdoor café where they were seated together. They had decided to leave the hayride to the kids, but they were nearby, keeping an eye on them.

"Everyone have a ticket?" Kyra asked, smirking a bit.

As everyone checked their pockets and bags and affirmed that they did, indeed, have their tickets, Kyra gave the thumbs-up.

"One time," Jacob started. "That happened to me *one time* at the water park last summer, and you won't let me live it down!"

The girls burst out laughing.

"I actually forgot all about that," Kyra assured him. "I promise I wasn't singling you out!"

"Uh-huh," Jacob replied. "Likely story." But he was smiling.

"I've never seen so much hay in my life," Grace said a moment later, gesturing with her arms to the stacks and stacks of hay bales all around the farm.

"I never realized hay could be so festive," Kyra added. "We should definitely take some selfies in front of the hay bales later."

"Selfies in front of the hay bales . . ." Miley repeated slowly. "That's a brilliant idea!"

"Well, thanks, but . . ." Kyra began.

"No, I mean for my party!" Miley laughed, her face lighting up into a huge grin. "We've been having a hard time securing a photo booth for my party—*surprise surprise*, the one we wanted wasn't available—and my mom and I were thinking we could do it ourselves, but I was trying to think of an awesome setting for the pictures. I just realized we can do hay bales! What do you think?"

"A hay bale photo booth?" JoJo nodded enthusiastically. "Love that idea!"

JoJo's phone pinged and she pulled it out of her pocket. She swiped the screen and read her text. "It's from Parker," she announced. "He's got some Hollywood gossip for us!"

"Oh, do tell!" Kyra said. Kyra loved Hollywood gossip almost as much as she loved fashion.

"It's about Lana . . ." JoJo began.

"Well, it must be good gossip if you're happy to share it," Grace commented.

"You know it!" JoJo said. There was no way she would want to spread negative gossip about anyone, let alone someone as sweet as Lana. And she was pretty sure Parker was the same way. "So apparently, Lana made it Instagram official just a few minutes ago that she's dating Frankie Delgado!"

"I love him!" Miley cried. "And I love his TV show!"

"Me too," JoJo agreed. "He seems like a really nice guy."

"He's so nice," Kyra said, nodding her head.

"Wait, do you know him or something?" Jacob asked, a confused look on his face.

"I don't have to know him *personally*," Kyra replied, rolling her eyes. "I've seen a million videos of him on YouTube, and he's definitely a good guy. I approve!"

"I'm sure Lana would be happy to know you approve," Jacob joked.

Everyone laughed, including Kyra, who was always up for some good-natured teasing.

"I think he must be her first real boyfriend," JoJo said as she dashed off a smiley-face emoji to Parker to let him know she'd seen his message. "I'm happy for her too. I bet they make a cute couple!"

"Look, they do!" Miley said, turning her phone around so the group could see a picture that popped up on her search engine.

Just then, Miley's phone pinged. She swiped her screen, an excited smile on her face. "It's my mom," she explained as she scanned the text. "We were supposed to hear back from the Mo's Candy Apples truck people about renting it for my party..."

Miley's voice trailed off, and JoJo saw her brow furrow.

"What's wrong?" JoJo asked.

Miley sighed and her shoulders slumped. "We can't get the truck. Apparently, some-one else rented it out for another party, so it's not available."

"Aw, I'm sorry," JoJo said sympathetically. "That's a bummer."

Miley sighed again and JoJo tried to think of something to say to cheer her up. She could tell her friends were also trying to come up with words of encouragement.

"Hey, Miley . . ." Jacob said slowly. "I was thinking . . . maybe I can crack the recipe for the candy apple coating Mo's uses and make candy apples for your party. I know it wouldn't be the same as the Mo's truck, but if you really wanted to have candy apples, I can definitely try to do it."

The smile on Miley's face was so bright that JoJo felt her own heart swell with happiness.

"That would be so amazing!" Miley cried. "Thank you so much, Jacob!"

"Don't thank me yet," Jacob cautioned. "I have to figure out the recipe first."

"If anyone can do it, you can!" Kyra cheered.

"I have total faith in you," Grace added. "And let us know how we can help."

"Actually . . ." Jacob began. "I think I *do* know how you can help. How about if we all go apple picking together? If I end up cracking the recipe, I'm gonna need a ton of apples! And then maybe you can help me with the dipping?"

"On it!" Grace responded. "I'll ask my mom if she can take us apple picking later this week."

"And I can help coordinate a dipping session," Kyra added. "Just let me know what you need."

"Now that's what I call teamwork," Miley said.

"Aww, group hug!" JoJo cried, pulling her friends in close. "You guys have me feeling all warm and fuzzy."

And then, finally, they were at the head of the line. A truck pulled up and a group of people who had just finished the hayride climbed down. One boy who looked to be about the same age as JoJo and her friends paused as he was about to pass them.

"I hope you like being scared, because that was *really* spooky . . ." he warned them.

"Awesome!" JoJo exclaimed.

"He was kidding, right? These things are usually pretty tame, aren't they?" Jacob asked as they surrendered their tickets to the teenager collecting them at the front of the line. Then they carefully climbed onto the back of the truck. They managed to secure a hay-covered bench all to themselves.

"I hope it's going to be scary," Miley replied as they settled into their seats. "That's the fun of it."

JoJo turned so she could see Jacob's face. He looked skeptical.

"Hey, it shouldn't be that bad, but if you're nervous, I'll jump off with you and we can go hang out at the café and wait for everyone else to get back," she whispered quietly so no one else could hear.

"You'd do that?" Jacob whispered back.

"Of course, I would," JoJo assured him. "What do you think?"

Jacob looked deep in thought for a moment. He sat up a little straighter and plastered a brave smile on his face. "Nah,

I'm good. It's just nerves. I can do this. But thanks, JoJo, I really appreciate it. Oh, and . . ."

JoJo waited for Jacob to finish his thought.

"I apologize in advance if I scream really loudly in your ear!"

CHAPTER 7

S oon they were off. The truck slowly rumbled over the gravelly road toward the woods. JoJo noticed for the first time how big the moon was in the night sky. It truly was the perfect fall night.

"I'm a little scared already," Grace whispered. She had her hands partially covering her eyes and was peeking out between her fingers.

"We've barely started moving," Kyra teased playfully. But a moment later, Kyra was the first one to let out a loud screech when a teenager in a mummy costume popped out from behind a tree.

"You were saying?" Grace giggled.

"Okay, you had the right idea." Kyra admitted as she huddled closer to Grace. "Jump scares always get me. Every time!"

JoJo looked at Jacob to make sure he wasn't too frightened, but he had an excited look on his face.

As the truck rumbled on, more teens dressed up in spooky costumes jumped out. JoJo saw ghosts, werewolves, skeletons, vampires, and more mummies. She wondered if they were going to see the zombies—that's what she was *most* looking forward to. Zombies were pretty much her favorite scary thing.

They went deeper into the woods and the moon hid behind tree branches, making it even darker. The jump scares were fun but not too scary, especially now that they were getting used to them, and everyone on the ride seemed to be having a great time. Miley was squeezing JoJo's hand so tightly that JoJo was pretty sure her fingers would be numb soon, but she was thrilled her friends seemed to be enjoying the hayride as much as she had hoped they would.

Then the truck stopped in a clearing deep in the woods. It was so quiet that JoJo could hear the breathing of her friends. Then she heard herself giggling nervously, and her friends soon joined in. What was going to happen next?

JoJo squinted in the dark and finally decided to use the flashlight feature on her phone to get a better look at their

surroundings. Several other people on the truck did the same, and soon a dozen thin beams of light helped to illuminate the area around them. JoJo could see there was a fake graveyard set up in the middle of the clearing with crumbling old headstones. The headstones had creepy names scrawled on them like U. R. NEXT and WILL B. SCARED. And the ground around the headstones looked like it had been freshly dug up!

"Psst, Miley—you should make note of the names on the headstones for your party decorations!" JoJo whispered.

"We hired someone to do the decorations, but that's still a good idea. Can you take notes for me though? I think I need to close my eyes," Miley whispered back. But JoJo could hear she was laughing, so she knew she wasn't *that* scared.

Then they all heard the low sound of moaning.

"I don't like the sound of that!" Miley squeaked as she buried her head on JoJo's shoulder.

"Those moans can only mean one thing," Jacob whispered. "Zombies!"

Jacob was right. Moments later, the first zombie made its appearance. It was wearing torn, loose-fitting clothes and had a blank stare on its creepy face. It shuffled slowly out from the trees and wandered around the clearing like it was in a daze. More zombies came out, shuffling slowly and moaning. Some were saying *brains* over and over again, which made JoJo and her friends laugh.

JoJo carefully studied the zombie costumes. She was definitely starting to feel spooked *and* inspired.

Then the hayride was almost over. Just as the truck neared the starting point, the driver pulled over and asked everyone on the ride to do him a favor and tell someone waiting in line how terrifying the ride was. "We like to get 'em good and scared before we start to set the tone!"

JoJo and Jacob exchanged a knowing look. So *that* was why that boy had warned them.

"I'm going to borrow that idea for my dad and uncle's Monster's Laboratory," Miley said. "Someone remind me to write it in my notebook! Along with the names from the headstones, just in case I need them, and of course my idea about the hay bale photo booth!"

As the truck parked and JoJo and her friends climbed down, they began to scan the crowd of people waiting to get on the next hayride.

"Can I do it?" Jacob asked the others. "I am feeling the urge to spread the scaries!"

The girls agreed. They decided it wouldn't be right to frighten any younger kids and instead chose a group of kids who looked to be teenagers. As they walked by, JoJo and her friends acted shaky, while Jacob paused and said, "Look, I feel like I should warn you that this ride is *super* scary! I mean, check out how scared my friends are!"

JoJo put her performance skills to good use and collapsed in a faux faint. Luckily Miley figured out what she was doing and caught her, and then the others helped to pretend-carry JoJo away. They waited until they were far enough away from the line before dissolving into gales of laughter.

"Okay, so I was barely even scared," Kyra said a moment later.

"Oh please, you had your eyes covered half the time!" Miley teased.

"Miley, you practically broke my fingers you were squeezing my hand so hard!" JoJo reminded her. "Even I had some freaked-out moments, and I never get scared!" Miley shrugged and playfully made a face.

"Who wants to get some hot apple cider before we leave?" Grace asked. She pointed to the outdoor café where JoJo and Kyra's moms were waiting.

"Great idea!" Kyra said. "Count me in."

"Me too," JoJo said.

"Me three," said Miley and Jacob in unison.

Moments later, JoJo and her friends were waiting for their steaming cups of hot apple cider to cool off.

"Say cheese!" JoJo motioned for everyone to pose for a group selfie and then texted the picture to Parker.

JUST WENT ON A SPOOKTACULAR HAUNTED HAYRIDE! WISH U WERE HERE!

A few seconds later, her phone pinged. Parker had replied with a sad face emoji and the message:

WISH I WAS THERE TOO!

"Aww, Parker's bummed he can't be here with us tonight," JoJo told the others.

"Tell him we say hi," Miley replied.

JoJo sent Parker a quick reply and slipped her phone back in her pocket. She took a tentative sip of the cider.

"Wow, that's yummy!" she commented. "Is that orange I'm tasting in there?"

"*That's it!*" Jacob shouted suddenly. He yelled it so loud that several people turned to stare at their group.

"It's all good over here!" JoJo smiled and waved.

"Jacob, what are you yelling about?" Kyra asked in a much quieter voice than Jacob had used.

"Orange!" he yelled. Then, realizing he was still yelling, he lowered his voice to a near whisper. "*Orange* is the special ingredient in the Mo's Candy Apples glaze. I'm sure of it! I think I just cracked the recipe!"

CHAPTER 8

The next morning JoJo woke up a little earlier than usual so she could work on planning the details of her costume. Halloween was just six days away, which meant Miley's party was five days away. JoJo had a lot of costume stuff to do and not a lot of time to do it! Luckily, she already had a pretty good idea of how to make her costume, and her mom's craft closet probably already had everything she needed and more.

BowBow was still snoozing next to JoJo's pillow as JoJo rose from bed and did some quick stretches to wake herself up. Bow-Bow let out an adorable little snore, which made JoJo giggle. But then, as she looked at her pup, she realized she actually had *two* costumes to make: one for her and one for BowBow.

"What do you want to be for Halloween, BowBow?" JoJo cooed. BowBow lifted her head and yawned. But her tail was thumping against the wall, so JoJo knew she was excited.

"How about a bumblebee?" JoJo asked. BowBow's tail thumped some more. "I think I like that idea too," JoJo told her. BowBow already had a black-and-yellow striped sweater she looked super cute in, so JoJo would just have to sew wings onto it. Bow-Bow's costume wouldn't be creepy, but JoJo's *definitely* would.

She had been so inspired by the creatures on the haunted hayride last night that she was now positive she could pull off a super creepy spin on her original idea: a peacock. But not just *any* peacock. A spooktacular one!

The peacock feathers were one of the most important parts of the costume, and maybe the most complicated too. JoJo knew she could pull together a great outfit to wear with the wings—she had a closet full of options from dance recitals and performances—but the exact outfit would have to wait until she figured out what her wings were going to look like. After all, a peacock's fan of feathers was its signature feature!

JoJo absently tapped her pink glitter pen against her notebook as she pondered. She had already done some research on how to make the feather fan, and there were two options: stiff fabric stretched over wire that would stand out on her back, or flowy fabric that would lay flat like a cape until she raised her arms. That style would attach to the arms of her outfit so that when she lifted them, the effect would be dazzling. After giving it a lot of thought, JoJo had decided she wanted to go with the flowy style, so she wouldn't have to worry about bumping people with them at the party. After all, JoJo planned to spend a lot of time on the dance floor and didn't want her feathers to get in the way. She had a pattern and instructions all set to go, but now she had to make an important decision: What fabric did she want to use?

She thought about the fabric she'd seen in her mom's crafting closet and decided to go check and see if there was enough there for her to make the wings.

A few minutes later, JoJo bit her lip in disappointment. According to the pattern she'd downloaded to her phone, she would need way more fabric than what was in the supply closet. She glanced at the clock on the wall. It was almost time for her to start her school lessons, but she was going to talk to her mom over breakfast. Hopefully, she would have an idea of where JoJo could find more fabric like this!

It turned out JoJo's mom knew just the place—Francesca's Fabrics, a fancy fabric store in Hollywood that carried all sorts of exotic and rare fabrics. "Even if they don't have that exact one, you should be able to find something special," her mom had promised. Apparently, famous costume designers shopped at Francesca's all the time.

That evening, JoJo and her mom drove to Francesca's. It was a fabric wonderland! JoJo had never seen so many gorgeous colors and patterns all in one place. The salesgirl asked if she could help them, and JoJo's mom showed her a small swatch of the fabric they were looking for.

"I don't have that exact one, but I think I have something similar," the girl said. "Give me a minute to go look in the back room!"

While they waited, JoJo reviewed the rest of her plans for her costume with her mom, who agreed that they had everything else she needed at home in the craft closet.

"But how exactly are you planning to make this a *scary* peacock?" her mom asked. "That's the part I'm not clear on! Peacocks are pretty, but not spooky."

"Oh, you see—" JoJo started to explain, but just then the salesgirl returned with a huge bolt of fabric.

"It's perfect!" JoJo cried, gently touching the silky, colorful patterned fabric. She loved that some of the colors were brighter shades, but there were enough darker colors that the overall effect was just somber enough that it would work perfectly for what she had in mind. "What do you think, Mom?"

"I agree it's beautiful," her mom nodded. "Let's get it!"

A few minutes later, JoJo and her mom were just finishing up at the register when a girl in a pink puffy jacket entered the store. Miley had the same jacket! And Miley had the same glittery purple headband this girl was wearing!

As they walked away from the register toward the door, JoJo's fabric carefully packaged in a gold shopping bag that said FRANCESCA'S FABRICS in fancy script, JoJo stopped in her tracks—the girl in the pink puffy jacket with the purple glitter head-band *was* Miley! She had just walked into Francesca's with *her* mom!

"Hey Miley," JoJo cried, running over to greet her best friend. "Fancy meeting you here!"

Miley burst out laughing as soon as she saw JoJo. "I guess this is what happens when we try to costume plan in secret—we bump into each other at the Hollywood fabric store your mom told my mom about!"

"That is too funny," JoJo said. "So, how's all the party stuff coming along?"

"Mostly good," Miley replied. "My mom found a place that can deliver tons of hay, so the hay bale photo booth is all set. The decorations, however, are another story. Would you believe the place we ordered decorations from canceled on us?"

"What?" JoJo exclaimed. "How can they do that?"

Miley shrugged. "Apparently they had a huge order placed for another party, and they thought they could do both but then realized they couldn't. I should have known everyone in LA would be throwing a Halloween party this weekend! They called my mom last night to cancel and offered us a discount on a future order."

"Ugh, that stinks," JoJo said. "But I'm sure we can come up with some great ideas—"

Miley held up her hand. "It's all good! We have it figured out. I think we can pull off some pretty amazing decorations with stuff from the party store. I told my mom about the graveyard we saw on the haunted hayride, and we're going to recreate something like that in my yard with headstones and cobwebs and hanging skeletons. Between that and all the hay bales, it will be super festive."

"That sounds perfect!" JoJo agreed. "I'm so glad the haunted hayride came through for you like that. I bet your decorations are going to be even better than the ones you had ordered!"

"I think so too," Miley agreed. "So other than that little bit of drama, everything else is working out. At least I hope so . . . because it does kind of seem like one thing after another has gone wrong with this party, and I'm not sure how many more issues I can take! Remind me next year to start planning *way* earlier!"

From the easygoing expression on her face, JoJo knew Miley was mostly kidding. Miley was the best, most careful planner JoJo knew! But the lead-up to her Halloween party had not been as smooth as it should have been. It was a good thing JoJo's BFF always kept such a positive attitude.

JoJo's mom glanced over, and JoJo could tell she was wrapping up her conversation with Miley's mom. "Real quick . . . let's take a selfie to send to Parker!" she said to Miley. "Since he basically grew up on movie sets, I'm sure he's heard of Francesca's." But when she pulled her phone out of her pocket, she saw she had a text from Jacob:

SOS! CANDY APPLE COATING RECIPE NOT WORKING OUT! WHAT IF I CAN'T PULL IT OFF? SHOULD I TELL MILEY?

JoJo hesitated. She wasn't sure if they should give Miley one more thing to worry about. After all, Jacob *always* came through when it came to recipes. She decided it wasn't worth troubling Miley just yet. If for whatever reason Jacob couldn't perfect the recipe, they would just figure something else out, like Miley had with the decorations and the music.

"Hang on, I just have another text I need to respond to really fast," JoJo said as she dashed off a quick reply to Jacob:

DON'T WORRY—IF ANYONE CAN CRACK THAT RECIPE, U CAN! LET'S JUST SEE WHERE U ARE BY THE TIME WE GO APPLE PICKING!

"Okay, done," JoJo said as she hit send and tapped the camera icon on her screen.

Miley leaned in, and JoJo held up the Francesca's bag with her free hand.

"Say *Halloween!*" Both girls hammed it up for the shot.

"It's perfect!" JoJo declared after checking the result. She texted the picture to Parker and captioned it:

UPPING THE ANTE FOR THE COSTUME CONTEST!

A few moments later Parker's response came in:

FRANCESCA'S? WHOA! STUFF JUST GOT REAL!

JoJo and Miley were laughing at his response when JoJo's phone pinged again. It was another text from Parker.

I WISH I COULD COMPETE IN THIS COSTUME CONTEST IN PERSON! ☹

"Aww," JoJo said. She showed Miley what Parker had said and noticed that Miley had a strange look on her face.

"What's the look?" JoJo asked Miley.

"What look?" Miley asked. But there was a gleam in her eye.

JoJo looked more closely at her best friend, and then the look was gone. JoJo must have imagined it.

CHAPTER 9

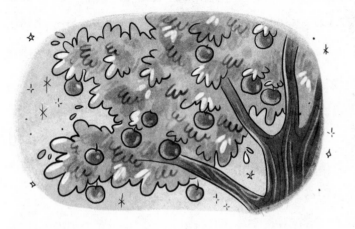

"How many apples are too many?" JoJo asked as she placed her giant bucket of apples next to Miley's and Grace's.

It was now just three days until Miley's party and four days until Halloween. JoJo, Miley, and Grace were at the orchard picking apples aplenty to bring to Jacob, who had rushed home from school to continue working on the recipe instead of joining the girls at the apple orchard.

"I think this is enough for sure," Miley said. "Once Jacob gets the candy glaze recipe perfected, we're going to have to spend every day leading up to the party dipping apples to have them ready in time!"

JoJo bit her lip. "Miley . . ." She began.

"Oh, it's okay." Miley waved a hand. "Jacob told me he was having issues with the recipe."

After a couple more days of recipe testing with a still-not-quite-right result, Jacob had decided it was time to let Miley know he was struggling with the recipe. Miley had taken the news in stride. Like JoJo, she was confident Jacob would pull it off. He almost always did!

"Well, I know Kyra said she'd coordinate a dipping party, but my costume is done, so I have plenty of free time," Grace offered, raising her hand. "Actually, Miley, that reminds me! Can I help out with your party decorations by painting some pumpkins you can put on display?"

"That would be great," Miley replied. "But only if you're sure you have time! And if you promise to make them spooky to stay on theme."

Grace gave her a thumbs-up. "I should have time to paint pumpkins *and* dip apples. And I'm sure Kyra will help too . . . though she was *very* mysterious about what she had to do tonight instead of coming with us! It must have been something costume-related, but I thought she finished her costume ages ago."

"I thought so too," Miley replied.

JoJo just smiled. She knew exactly why Kyra wasn't there, and it *was* costume-related. But it was related to Grace's costume! Kyra had texted JoJo the night before to say she'd had a fabulous idea of how to make Grace's unicorn horn even more special—it involved hand-placed crystals in a swirling pattern over the rainbow glitter. Kyra wanted to finish the horn so she could give it to Grace today in case she actually was planning to dress up as a unicorn for the party. JoJo had been sworn to secrecy, and there was no way she was going to spill the beans! She loved surprises and couldn't wait to see Grace's face when Kyra revealed hers!

JoJo decided to steer the conversation away from Kyra, just in case Grace was getting suspicious. "I heard from Parker today, and he claims his costume is the best one he's ever had," JoJo said. "I've been trying to get him to slip and reveal a hint, but it's not working. He's super good at secret keeping!"

Miley laughed and then clamped her mouth closed.

"Why was that funny?" JoJo asked. She looked at Grace, who just shrugged.

"Sorry, I was thinking about something else," Miley said. JoJo noticed her face was a little red. "Be right back—I'm going to go check out the muffins they're selling over there!"

With that, Miley bolted away and headed over to the orchard's display of home-baked goods.

JoJo looked at Grace. "Is it just me or is Miley acting a little . . . strangely? Does she have a crush on Parker or something? She blushes every time his name comes up!"

"She seems fine to me," Grace said after giving it a moment's consideration. "I think she is just excited about the party and still has a lot to do to pull it together. But maybe she has a crush—who knows?"

JoJo nodded. Grace was probably right. Miley *did* have an awful lot going on. And JoJo certainly knew what that was like. If

Miley had a crush on Parker, she'd tell her when she was ready.

A little while later, Grace's mom dropped the girls off at Jacob's house. Kyra had planned to meet them there—her dad's car was pulling away just as they arrived.

"How'd it go?" Kyra asked, rushing over to take a bag of apples from Grace, who was struggling under the weight of two paper bags filled to the brim. "Never mind—I can see your trip was a success!"

"It definitely was," JoJo agreed as they headed into Jacob's house. She led the way into the cozy kitchen, where she was pretty sure they would find Jacob. And she was right! Jacob was indeed in the kitchen, wearing his favorite blue apron that the girls had all given him for his birthday a few months ago. But JoJo could tell almost immediately that something wasn't quite right. The

kitchen was an absolute disaster! There were bowls piled high in the sink, pools of spilled ingredients on the countertops . . . and Jacob looked positively exhausted!

The girls set the bags down on the kitchen table and rushed over to Jacob.

"What's going on?" JoJo asked gently. "I've never seen your kitchen look . . . like *this*. Are you okay?"

Jacob sighed and took off his apron, folding it and stashing it on the counter. He gestured for his friends to sit down at the kitchen table.

"I can't crack the recipe," Jacob said glumly once everyone was seated. "I still think orange is the secret ingredient, but I can't figure out how to make it work. I've tried orange juice, orange zest, orange puree, orange flavoring . . . none of them are right."

"Do you like any of the versions you came up with?" Grace asked.

Jacob shrugged. "Sure, some of them taste okay . . . but they taste like every other candy apple you've ever had. Not special. I really wanted to crack that recipe to make them special for Miley's party."

JoJo saw Miley's face fall, and she knew Miley probably felt awful that Jacob was putting so much pressure on himself.

"First of all, anything you make and bring to my party would be special simply because you made it," Miley said firmly. "But you don't even have to bring *anything*! The most important thing to me is that you're there and you have an amazing time!"

"But I feel like I'm letting you down," Jacob sighed. "I really wanted you to have those incredible candy apples at your party, since you couldn't get the Mo's truck."

"You so are *not* letting me down!" Miley assured him. She looked at JoJo for backup, and JoJo nodded.

"Jacob, don't be so hard on yourself," JoJo said. "Mo's Candy Apples are famous for a reason. They are one of a kind. That's why the recipe is so hard to crack—it's totally top-secret! The secret ingredient is probably something crazy like . . . ketchup!"

"Now that *would* be crazy," Jacob replied, cracking a smile. "Not to mention disgusting!"

"Or maybe the secret ingredient is pickle juice!" Kyra said, and everyone laughed.

"Or pumpkin puree!" Grace added. "Which is probably only gross to me, but you know what I mean!"

"Hmm, I never thought of pumpkin," Jacob said. He started to jump up from his seat, and all four girls rose from theirs.

"Jacob, it's time for some tough love," Kyra began. She put her hands on her hips. "Let it go! You are the best dessert chef any of us know—you make the best pies, cookies, donuts, cakes, and muffins I've ever had. So what if you can't make the perfect candy apple glaze? It's really not the end of the world, or even the end of Halloween! Miley's party will go on, and it will all be okay."

"I *do* make really good donuts," Jacob agreed. His eyes wandered to the bags of apples on the table. "Miley, how about if I make another apple-based treat for your party?"

"That would be amazing," Miley lit up. "But only if you want to! And only if your costume is finished and you have enough time to do it."

"I have plenty of time," Jacob said confidently. But then his face clouded over again. "My costume is another story. I haven't even figured out what I want to be."

"Probably because you've been spending so much time in the kitchen," Kyra said.

"Do you have any ideas at all?" Grace asked.

Jacob just shrugged. "A candy apple?" he said miserably.

"We're here for you if you need help," JoJo assured him. "I mean, we can break the secrecy pact if need be to help Jacob come up with a costume, right?"

"Absolutely!" Miley, Kyra, and Grace all said in unison.

"Thanks," Jacob said, nodding distractedly as his eyes scanned the kitchen. "I'll let you know . . ." From the way his voice trailed off, JoJo had a feeling that inspiration had struck and an idea was taking shape in Jacob's head. She just hoped he wasn't really planning to dress up as a candy apple because that would be really, *really* sticky.

"Well, speaking of costumes . . ." Kyra said a moment later. She caught JoJo's eye, and JoJo knew exactly what was coming next. "I have a quick surprise for Grace. Give me one second to go get it!"

"A surprise for me?" Grace repeated as Kyra walked away. "Does anyone know what it is?"

"I do!" JoJo exclaimed. "And you're gonna love it!"

Kyra returned a moment later and held out a rainbow-colored gift bag to Grace. "This is a little something I made for you to help make your costume extra-special. That is, if your costume is what I think it is. But even if it's not, I hope you love it anyway! Happy early Halloween!"

Grace giggled excitedly as she dug through the tissue paper, finally pulling out the handmade unicorn horn. It was even more spectacular than JoJo had imagined it would be! The tall, shimmering horn was covered in rainbow glitter. And the swirling crystals put it over the top to make it truly extraordinary!

"I love it so much!" Grace cried. "And it actually *does* work with my costume—but my costume is not a unicorn, believe it or not. Not exactly anyway!"

"Not a unicorn, but the horn still works?" Jacob repeated. "That's a head-scratcher."

"You'll see soon enough," Grace promised. Then she turned back to Kyra. "Thank you so much! You're the best BFF in the whole world!"

The two friends hugged, and JoJo pulled out her phone to snap a quick picture. This was a moment she wanted to remember.

Soon it was time to head home. Grace's mom was driving Kyra home, and she offered to bring JoJo home too.

"Thanks, but I'm going home with Miley, and my mom is going to pick me up there in a little bit," JoJo replied.

Back at Miley's, the two girls had a snack in the kitchen while JoJo waited for her mom to arrive.

"So, we're in the final countdown to the party," JoJo said as she sipped lemonade. "Do you need me to make any last-minute changes to the playlist I sent you?"

Miley shook her head. "Nope, it was perfect. The music is all set, and it's going to be amazing!"

"So you tested out Kyra's dad's speakers and they sound okay?" JoJo asked.

For a moment, Miley looked confused, but then she nodded. "Oh yeah . . . her dad's speakers are really high quality. Like I said, the music is going to be amazing!"

The girls chatted for a few more minutes, and then JoJo heard her mom honk the car horn to let her know she'd arrived. JoJo jumped up from her chair and gave Miley a quick hug goodbye. The next time they saw each other would be at the party!

CHAPTER 10

JoJo glanced at the clock on her nightstand one more time—it was almost time to get ready for Miley's party! In previous years, JoJo had gotten ready for the big bash at Miley's house and had helped her set everything up. This year, since they were surprising each other with their costumes, JoJo, Kyra, Grace, and Jacob were getting ready at their own homes and heading over to Miley's a bit early so they could do their costume reveals together just before the party started.

JoJo was brimming with excitement about everything the next several hours had in store: seeing her friends in their costumes, seeing Miley's graveyard decorations, dancing to the amazing playlist they had pulled together, visiting Miley's dad's Monster's Laboratory in the basement, seeing Parker's costume on Snapchat . . . and of course, the costume contest itself! The list went on and on! And that didn't even take into account the fact that tomorrow was Halloween, and that meant trick-or-treating with her friends!

Finally, it was officially time to start getting ready. Already dressed in the black unitard that was the base of her costume, JoJo decided to tackle her makeup first. Makeup was what would turn her costume into something extra-spooky and special!

JoJo took a deep breath and headed into the bathroom, which had the best lighting for what she needed to do. She already had all of her makeup supplies spread out on the counter. She'd watched a bunch of makeup tutorials online and had been practicing the look she wanted to achieve—plus an extra-special JoJo flair, of course—so she knew just what to do. With her hair already styled—she had it pulled into a side-pony so it was off her face—she first applied a gray-tinged cream to her face to make herself look ghostly pale. Next, she used a deeper gray cream to create deep shadows under her eyes. Using a thick red face paint, she carefully painted the finishing touches. But because she was still JoJo, she topped it off with a dusting of glitter and a heart around her eye. Just because her costume was creepy, didn't mean she couldn't have a little bit of sparkle. She hoped her friends would be able to tell what she was!

Next came the feathers. JoJo and her mom had worked really hard on her bedazzled wings and she was thrilled with how they had turned out. She slipped them over her arms and then and wrapped a tattered black skirt around her waist over her unitard. Finally, she placed a headband she had made to resemble a peacock's plumage on her head.

JoJo stepped in front of her mirror. She turned to one side and then the other. She practiced her best scary face, and then burst out laughing—it was hard to look frightening when she felt so excited and happy! Deciding everything was just right with her costume, she headed downstairs so her mom could snap a few pictures and then take her to Miley's. She couldn't wait to see her friends and get the party started!

"**W**elcome to our home . . . enter at your own risk!"

"You look great, Mr. Taylor!" JoJo exclaimed. "That's a super creepy vampire costume!"

Miley's dad sighed and pulled out his fake fangs. "You recognized me right away and didn't seem scared at all! What'd I do wrong? Do I need to work on my Transylvanian accent?"

"No, your accent was spot-on!" JoJo assured him. "But Miley had told me you were going to be a vampire. I'm sure you will terrify everyone else. I can't wait to visit your Monster's Laboratory later!"

Mr. Taylor grinned and popped his fangs back in. "Excellent! The gang is up in Miley's room. I've been instructed to send all other guests to the yard where the party is so that your crew can do a private costume reveal upstairs."

JoJo thanked him and headed upstairs. BowBow, who was looking adorable in her bumblebee costume, was curled up in her arms, her tail thumping happily. She had been to Miley's house many times before and seemed excited to be back. JoJo could hear her friends' voices inside Miley's room, so she slowly opened the door and entered.

The next thing JoJo knew, a pair of hands were covering her eyes! JoJo yelped out in fright until she heard Miley's familiar snorting chuckle.

Miley had snuck up on JoJo from behind! JoJo felt herself relax as Miley gently removed her hands from her eyes.

"Turn around on the count of three?" Miley asked.

"One, two . . ." JoJo began to count.

"THREE!" JoJo spun around and let out a delighted shriek. It took her a moment to figure out who was who because their costumes were so fantastic. As she took it all in, she paused to put BowBow down. The little pup began running around in circles excitedly.

Miley was the glitteriest mermaid JoJo had ever seen! She had found the most perfect iridescent blueish-green material for her costume. JoJo's favorite part of the whole costume, though, was the way Miley had styled her hair, sweeping it into a long, flowing cascade over one shoulder with little shell barrettes scattered all around. She looked positively beautiful.

Grace's cat-icorn costume was absolutely adorable! She wore a fuzzy, rainbow-colored onesie that JoJo thought was a brilliant use of cozy pajamas, and had sprayed her long red ponytail with rainbow colors so it looked like a unicorn's flowing mane. Kyra's special horn was nestled on her head and it looked spectacular. Cat ears and whiskers transformed the costume from a *unicorn* into a *caticorn*.

Kyra was the most fabulous looking disco dancer—her sparkly gold dress and tall white boots were absolutely perfect, which was not at all surprising given that Kyra was their resident fashionista! Glittery makeup and dangling disco ball earrings completed the look.

And Jacob's costume . . . JoJo had to take a step back to get a better look.

"Jacob, your costume . . ." JoJo tried to find the right words. "I would say it's totally bananas, but instead I will say it's totally DONUTS!"

JoJo could hardly believe it, but Jacob had dressed up as a *donut vending machine*! "Please tell me it actually works," JoJo begged.

"Try it and see," Jacob said, stepping forward. "Remember I said I had a special, apple-based treat I was going to make in place of the candy apples?"

JoJo pulled the lever on the side of his costume and a moment later an apple cider donut slid out and landed on the platter Jacob was holding.

"That is so brilliant!" JoJo exclaimed, taking a giant bite and uttering a satisfied *mmmm*. "You all look SO GOOD! It was totally worth the surprise of waiting to see your costumes! I mean, it was basically torture but so worth it. Any one of you could win the costume contest; you look that good. And—"

"JoJo, stop talking!" Kyra commanded, playfully holding a hand up. "Let us all look at this amazing costume you have on and figure out what exactly you are!"

"Oh right!" JoJo laughed. She took a step back and held out her arms to showcase her wings in all their glory. Then she made her best undead face.

"OMG! You're a zombie peacock!" Miley cried. "I love it so much!"

"You got it!" JoJo clapped excitedly, spoiling the creep factor.

"What a creative idea!" Grace cheered. "Check out that gash on your cheek and your amazing makeup art! You're definitely gonna win the contest with that costume! You'll get my vote for sure."

"And what about BowBow?" JoJo asked, pointing to the floor where BowBow stood, tail a-wag.

"BowBow is the cutest bumblebee ever," Miley cooed. "Who knows, maybe she will win the contest!"

130

"Nope, I'm not gonna enter her," JoJo laughed. "I was actually wondering if it would be okay to keep her up here until after the contest? That way I can be hands-free to try all the snacks, and then BowBow can make her big debut later in the night."

"Of course," Miley agreed.

"Speaking of the contest . . ." Miley hugged her arms around herself excitedly. "Let's go outside. Some guests should have started to arrive by now and let's just say . . . I have some surprises in store!"

As the friends headed downstairs, JoJo could hear music and party sounds coming from outside. It sounded like the party was indeed well underway.

"Wow, those speakers really are professional quality," JoJo said to Miley as they stepped into Miley's yard. She craned her neck to try to catch a glimpse of the sound system, but Miley's huge backyard was too crowded with people to be able to see it. And then JoJo forgot all about the sound system for a moment as she took in the decorations, which were out of this world!

"Miley, I know you and your mom are really good at crafting, but these decorations look beyond professional," JoJo said. "I can't believe you pulled this off with stuff from the party store! It looks like a spooky movie set out here! And wow, look at all the hay bales! They really do look awesome . . ."

Miley nodded happily. She was so excited she was bouncing up and down. "Why don't you mingle for a little while and try some snacks? I have to refill the candy bowl, so I'll be right back."

JoJo nodded and began to scope out the guests at the party. She recognized a few of the kids there, having met Miley's classmates at her previous parties, though several took her a moment to recognize because of their Halloween costumes. As she walked around, JoJo waved and said hello to the others. There were so many great costumes! JoJo took selfies with a pirate, a pretty ballerina, and a creepy clown. Everyone seemed to want a selfie with her, and she was happy to do it.

Just as JoJo was about to approach two girls she didn't recognize to introduce herself, she spotted a really spooky-looking ghost lurking in a dark corner of the deck, near one of the main snack tables. The ghost's costume was amazing—he or she wore a flowing, nearly transparent white robe with a hood totally covering their head. The robe seemed to sway in the gentle evening breeze, and the effect was very creepy—it didn't look like anyone was underneath! Whoever made that costume knew a thing or two about choosing the right fabric. It was impossible to see the ghost's face because of the hood. As JoJo tried to place which of Miley's friends it might be, the two girls she had noticed before approached her, wearing warm smiles. JoJo realized they looked vaguely familiar, but she couldn't quite place them.

"Hi, I'm JoJo!" she said, waving to the girls. "Have we met before? You both look a little familiar to me—" JoJo stopped as it hit her. They were both backup dancers for pop stars she loved! "You're Cameron, and you're Reese, right? You're both so talented!"

"Thanks, JoJo." Reese—who was dressed as a black cat—grinned. "We're big fans of yours too! That's why we wanted to come say hello."

"How do you know Miley?" JoJo asked.

"Oh, we just met her tonight," Cameron, who was dressed as a pumpkin, replied.

Before JoJo could ask them why they were at Miley's party, she felt someone tug on her arm. "It was nice meeting you both," she called as she was pulled away.

She turned to face Miley, who was grinning from ear to ear.

"So, have you figured it out yet?" Miley asked.

"I am so confused," JoJo admitted. "I have that feeling I get on Christmas morning before I open all my presents where I know something amazing is coming . . . but I am trying to pull this all together, and I'm stumped. This party is totally over-the-top! How did you get TV stars here? And how—" Just then, JoJo spotted the ghost again as they continued to lurk around the snack table, coming out from the shadows every now and then, only to quickly retreat back as soon as JoJo looked over. JoJo shivered. Why did it seem like the ghost was trying to get her attention?

"Do you know who that is?" JoJo asked, gesturing to the ghost.

"Why don't you go find out?" Miley said, her eyes twinkling. "I think it will explain a lot!"

And then it dawned on JoJo. Was the ghost *Parker?* It had to be! But how was he at Miley's party? What about Lana's party?

JoJo marched over to the ghost, who turned to face her but still said nothing.

"Okay, it's time to unveil yourself, Parker," JoJo said. "And I have to tell you, this costume is absolutely amazing. You really outdid yourself. What I can't figure out is, how are you here? How could you miss Lana's party?"

As JoJo waited, the ghost slowly slid its hood down. "I knew it—" JoJo started to say.

And then she stopped talking and her mouth hung open for a moment in amazement, as her brain tried to make sense of what she saw in front of her.

The ghost was *not* Parker.

CHAPTER 11

"**W**ait! What? How?" JoJo shouted as Lana Marks burst into laughter from beneath her ghostly hood and leaned forward to give JoJo a big hug.

"Happy Halloween! Surprise!" Lana exclaimed.

"To say the least," JoJo said as Miley appeared at her side. "Explain, please!"

"Do you want to, or shall I?" Lana asked Miley.

"Go for it," Miley replied.

"Well, Parker reached out to me after Miley reached out to him," Lana began. "He told me that Miley had this great idea that we could combine our two parties into one huge party so we could all be together. I thought it was an amazing idea, and so here we are! Parker didn't want to miss out on Miley's party, and it's so fun to have us all together for Halloween!"

JoJo looked at Miley. "How on earth did you ever come up with that idea?"

"The idea actually came to me that night we bumped into each other at Francesca's," Miley explained. "Remember when Parker texted that he wished he could compete at the costume contest in person?"

JoJo nodded.

"Well, that got me thinking about combining the parties. I know you kept saying you didn't mind missing Lana's party for mine, but I felt bad about it." When JoJo started to protest, Miley held up a hand to stop her. "You never made me feel bad about it, but I *know* how important your movie is and how much you would have loved to be there with the rest of the cast, so I figured it couldn't hurt to ask Parker if he thought Lana might go for it. Plus, what better way to promote the movie than having all the cast together taking selfies and having fun!"

JoJo turned to Lana. "Didn't you mind, though?" Her head was spinning as she tried to take it all in. She couldn't believe Miley had done this for her—and that Lana had agreed.

"Not at all," Lana replied smoothly. "I was really bummed you couldn't come to my party, even though I definitely understood why you couldn't miss your BFF's party. But we really wanted the whole cast to be there, so this was the perfect solution. We decided to bring the party to you, since we wanted to surprise you!"

"Okay, this is beyond awesome!" JoJo said as she looked around.

"Besides, I had way too many candy apples for my party," Lana continued, gesturing to where a Mo's Candy Apples tent was being set up on the back of the property.

"Miley! You got the apples you wanted after all!" JoJo exclaimed.

"I got the apples and more!" Miley grinned. "When Lana and I realized the reason I couldn't get the candy apple truck . . . we put two and two together. The DJ I wanted and the party decorations were booked for *her* party! It made even more sense at that point to combine the two parties. Now we have all that stuff and more." Miley turned to Lana and gave her a one-armed hug. "Thanks so much for agreeing to do this.

Not only did you help make my BFF super happy, but this is basically my dream Halloween party!"

"Mine too," Lana said. "And you know what my favorite part is? The hay bale photo booth you have here. I never would have thought of that on my own, but we can get the coolest promo shots there, and I can post them to Insta. Miley, you truly are the hostess with the mostest!"

"Well if Miley's the hostess with the mostest, then you're the *ghostess* with the mostest!" JoJo joked. As her eyes wandered around the yard, something occurred to her. "Hey, wait a second! Speaking of Parker, where is he? Now that I know he's not the ultra-creepy ghost, I need to see his costume."

"He wants to wait and make a grand entrance during the contest," Lana explained. "But I know what it is, and you won't be let down!"

JoJo looked at Miley, who shrugged. "He wouldn't give me any hints."

JoJo scoped out the crowd some more, looking for someone as tall as Parker, but she didn't see anyone she thought could be him.

"Oh, hey, did you bring your pup, Bow-Bow?" Lana asked, "I've always wanted to meet her!"

JoJo nodded. "She's up in Miley's room. I was planning to bring her down after the costume contest, but I can go get her now."

"No worries," Lana waved a hand. "But I have to run inside to get my phone. Okay if I drop by to say hello to her?"

"Sure thing," JoJo agreed. "She's super friendly. Just make sure you tell her you love her bumblebee costume."

A few minutes later, the DJ announced the costume contest was beginning. JoJo was glad to see that Lana had returned from her visit with BowBow and was back outside.

JoJo, Miley, and Lana got in the line for the contest, joining Kyra, Grace, and Jacob and scores of other kids. As Miley introduced Lana to their friends, JoJo looked around again for Parker. She couldn't find him anywhere. Could his costume be that good that she couldn't even recognize him?

"Wait, you painted those pumpkins over there?" Lana was saying to Grace.

Grace nodded. "Yep! I finished my costume earlier this week and had some free time, so I painted pumpkins for Miley to use as decorations at her party. Of course, that was before I knew she was going to have the professional decorations from *your* party!"

"Those pumpkins are one of the best parts," Lana replied. "You're seriously talented."

"See, I told you they were awesome," Kyra whispered to Grace, who was sporting the proudest smile JoJo had ever seen.

As they got closer and closer to the head of the line, JoJo dashed off a quick text to Parker:

WHERE ARE U? COSTUME CONTEST HAPPENING NOW!

Kyra, Jacob, Miley, Grace, and Lana strutted out to show off their costumes. Jacob made the most of his moment, tossing out donuts to the cheering crowd.

Then it was JoJo's turn. She made her best scary zombie face but couldn't hold it for very long without dissolving into laughter. Everyone gasped when she spread her arms out to show off her beautiful bedazzled wings. She got a ton of cheers and applause.

As JoJo joined her friends near the candy apple tent, the DJ paused the dance music and played drum roll. "And now, for *my* favorite costume of the night . . ." the DJ began in a dramatic voice. "Here's Parker Lawrence dressed up as . . . well, you just have to see this for yourself!"

JoJo rushed toward the front of the crowd so she could get a good look at Parker's costume as he came strutting out.

"No way!" JoJo exclaimed, then burst out laughing. Parker's costume was truly *the best*.

He approached center stage, wearing a huge smile on his face and sporting a blond wig pulled back into a side-pony and secured with a rainbow hair bow. He twirled once in his glittery skirt and took a bow.

Parker was the spitting image of *JoJo*!

To top it all off, he was even carrying bumblebee BowBow in his arms.

JoJo's friends rushed to her side and doubled over in laughter, as the crowd went crazy for Parker's costume.

"I told you, you wouldn't be disappointed!" Lana said between fits of laughter.

"That's why you wanted to know where BowBow was!" JoJo realized.

"Guilty as charged," Lana laughed. "Though I did really want to meet her too."

"Can I get the real JoJo Siwa up here for a picture?" the DJ asked.

JoJo happily ran up to where Parker was standing. "This is hilarious, and you look amazing!" she told him. "But give me Bow-Bow back! My poor baby must be totally confused!"

A few minutes later, after everyone at the party got all the pictures they wanted of the real JoJo and the costumed JoJo—BowBow tucked in the middle—it was time to announce the winner of the costume contest.

"And the winner is . . ." The DJ played another drumroll. JoJo was sure it would be Parker. The guests held their breaths.

"Without further ado . . ."

"I can't stand the suspense," Miley remarked.

The DJ whipped out a card with a flourish and read the note inside. "I give you . . . the donut vending machine!"

"Jacob, you won!" JoJo shouted, jumping up and down. "Way to go!"

"Handing out donuts was a brilliant move," Parker whispered to JoJo, as Jacob ran up to collect his prize. "I'm going to have to incorporate a food item into next year's costume."

"Shh," JoJo laughed. "I want to hear this!"

Miley and Lana were standing next to the DJ with their arms linked as cohostesses of the party, waiting to give Jacob his prize. Lana borrowed the microphone from the DJ and stepped forward.

"Not only does Jacob get bragging rights, he also gets an awesome prize," Lana began.

"In fact, the artist behind the prize is in the crowd. Can we get her up here too?"

As the crowd cheered, Miley pulled Grace up to join them. Grace pulled Kyra up with her.

"I'm not sure you knew what you were getting yourself into now that you have to paint a donut vending machine!" Lana joked to Grace. "But kidding aside, those hand-painted pumpkins you made are beautiful, and as the winner of the contest, Jacob is lucky to get one! Kudos to both of you! Why don't you both say a few words?"

"Thank you." Grace stepped forward and spoke into the microphone. "And thank you to my best friend, Kyra, for encouraging me to paint the pumpkins. She's always super supportive of my art! I can't wait to paint Jacob a special pumpkin as his reward."

"And thank you everyone for this honor," Jacob said, stepping forward to speak into the microphone. JoJo was pretty sure she had never seen him look happier. "I'm not sure if I won because you all really loved my costume or my donuts . . . but I'll take the win either way! And I would also like to say thank you to my best friends for supporting me!"

"Yay, us!" Kyra cheered, and everyone cracked up laughing.

"Now that's a group I need a picture of," JoJo said, pulling out her phone. She snapped a picture of her closest friends: Miley, Kyra, Grace, and Jacob, with her newest friends Lana and Parker.

"Do you have anything to add?" Lana asked Miley.

Miley nodded and Lana handed her the microphone. "Umm . . . I just wanted to thank everyone for coming and say thank you to Lana for combining parties. I hope you're all having as much fun as I am! Now let's all go eat snacks, dance, pose for pics at the photo booth, visit the Monster's laboratory in the basement and . . ." Miley paused and pulled Lana to her side. Together the two girls shouted into the microphone, "*Have a spooktacular Halloween!*"

Everyone erupted in cheers. Then, as the crowd dispersed and the music came back on, Lana appeared at JoJo and Parker's side.

"Ready for some cast photos?" she asked. "Let's start with some shots by the hay bales before they get totally mobbed by everyone else."

JoJo and Parker posed for a series of shots with each other, with their costars, and of course with Lana. Lana quickly edited and posted the pictures as they went. JoJo could tell Lana was an extremely experienced social media influencer.

"The one of you two with BowBow has already gotten a bajillion likes," Lana exclaimed to JoJo and Parker. "Everyone is going crazy over real JoJo and faux JoJo."

"And . . . that's your new nickname," JoJo told Parker. "FauxJo!"

"We'll see about that," Parker replied. But he was laughing.

Just then, the song that had been playing ended and a new one began. It was JoJo's hit "Kid in a Candy Store."

"That," JoJo said, a huge grin lighting up her face, "is our cue to hit the dance floor and really get this party started! Maybe with candy apples in hand." She winked.

As JoJo and her friends, new and old, took to the dance floor, JoJo couldn't imagine a more perfect evening. Or a more perfect Halloween party.

MORE BOOKS AVAILABLE . . .

. . . BY JOJO SIWA!